5/18

D0842736

HSUS The Humane Society
of the United States

Ruffle, Coo
and Hoodoo

by Randy Houk

*To Susan and Elaine, who
gave endless encouragement.*

Based on a true story

The Benefactory, Inc.

In a forest far away,
Monkeys call and tall trees sway.
Two young parrots dance and play,
Dance together, dance away.

Parrots mate for life, they say,
Once they choose, they choose to stay.
They don't stray. They don't get jealous -
If they do, they never tell us.

Each picks one he likes a lot.
Each sticks with the one she's got.
One blue parrot, one bright green,
Screech and chatter, dance and preen.

Parrots with long tails are named
'Parakeets,' if wild or tamed.
These are both 'monk parakeets,'
One foot long, from tail to beaks.

Feathers spread, the birds 'display.'
Closer now, their names they say.
"I'm called 'Ruffle'" – "I'm called 'Coo.'"
(Coo is green and Ruffle blue.)

Sunlight falls in spots of yellow.
Somewhere near, a jaguar's bellow.
One blue parrot, one bright green,
Screech and chatter, dance and preen.

Near the courting parakeets,
Hunters creep on silent feet.
Blue monk parakeets are rare -
Ruffle wasn't taking care.

Through the jungle, hunters glide.
Just behind the birds they slide -
Then the net comes crashing down.
Ruffle's trapped, without a sound.

Coo flaps frantically about.
"**Go**," screams Ruffle. "Fly. Get out."
Coo won't leave his mate. He flies,
Diving, for the hunters' eyes.

Then the hunters swing at Coo.
Soon enough, they've trapped him too.
Wings are clipped and feet are tied.
Ruff and Coo are terrified.

6

From the forest, green and gracious,
From the forest, lush and spacious,
Come the parrots, stuffed in crates,
Bound for pet stores in the States.

To New York the crates are flown.
Coo and Ruffle screech and moan.
Coo and Ruffle, and some others,
Taken from their friends and mothers.

In New York, a burly man
Loads the crates into a van.
Ruffle squawks - the van is airless -
And the burly man gets careless.

And a crate falls, with a crash.
Fifty birds fly in a flash.
Green and blue and yellow feathers,
Winging through New England weathers.

Sudden freedom is a shock -
But the parrots form a flock.
On they fly, without a rest,
Looking for a place to nest.

*O*n they fly, and reach a city,
Kind of grimy, kind of gritty.
Smokestacks turn the air to brown,
Garbage floats upon the Sound.

Near the harbor, there's a tree.
It's been there a century,
Tall and leaning in the breeze
Blowing, blowing off the seas.

Standing graceful, proud and high,
To that tree the parrots fly.
One by one, the birds alight.
Somehow, this tree feels just right.

Ruffle perches on a twig.
Coo hops on a branch that's big,
Looking for the branch that's best,
Just the branch to hold their nest.

Ruffle gives a happy 'squawk,'
Telling Coo, in parrot talk,
She has found a branch that's strong -
Just the branch where they belong.

9

Neighbors hear the parrots chatter.
Underneath the tree they gather.
"Look at that," the neighbors mutter,
As the parrots chirp and flutter.

"Here in Bridgeport! Did you ever."
Say the neighbors. "Well, I never!
Look! They're getting twigs and sticks.
Aren't they clever. Aren't they quick."

"Aren't they noisy!" says a fellow.
"What a screech. I have to bellow.
Do we want them building nests?
Might those parrots be pure pests?"

"They won't stay," the neighbors say.
"They'll be gone by break of day.
Those are not New England birds.
They'll move on. Just mark my words."

Golden light spills over all.
Purple shadows creep and crawl.
All the neighbors disappear.
Coo and Ruffle huddle near.

Close and still and safe all night,
Not a sound, till dawn's first light.
Then the nesting starts once more
In the tree above the shore.

Ruffle carries sticks and things,
Coo weaves in what Ruffle brings.
Several others come help too -
They will nest with Ruff and Coo.

"How can those birds stand our winter?"
Ask the neighbors. "It's so bitter.
Ice and snow - how can they take it?
Mark my words. Those birds won't make it."

Coo and Ruffle, working fast,
Want a nest that's going to last.
Something tells them, build it thick.
Build it strong, and build it quick.

Two days later, drenching rain
Brings a howling hurricane.
Wind and sleet pound parrot nests,
But their work withstands the tests.

Coo and Ruffle, safe within,
Listen to the crashing din,
Think they'll add a twig or two
When the hurricane is through.

Fall sends painted leaves aswirl.
On the winds, they dance and twirl.
Morning fog and mist curl 'round
Off the cold Long Island Sound.

Winter comes, and snow drifts high.
In the branches, cold winds sigh.
In their nests, the parrots huddle.
Coo and Ruffle dream and cuddle.

Icy winds make branches quiver.
In their nests, the parrots shiver.
Seeds and buds are hard to find.
Winter here is quite unkind.

Then the coldest months are past.
Most birds make it - most birds last.
Coo and Ruffle, young and strong,
Do just fine, all winter long.

*L*ate one chilly winter night,
As the moon spills silver light,
Two dark shadows drift like ghosts.
Down into the tree they float.

Coo is restless. He can't sleep.
He wakes Ruffle with a 'peep.'
Something's out there, they agree.
Better not go out and see.

In the morning, neighbors speak.
"Look. A parrot's foot and beak.
What on earth could hunt and eat
A thirteen inch parakeet?"

Coo and Ruffle screech and squawk.
Warn the flock, in parrot talk,
"When night falls, you'd better hide.
It's not safe out. Stay inside."

All the birds wheel 'round in fright,
But they settle at twilight.
They won't leave their tree. Not now –
They've got nests here anyhow.

Now against the moon's pale face,
Something launches into space.
Dark on dark, the hunter flies.
"Whooo - who-whooooo - who-whooooo," it cries.

"Whoooo," another owl replies,
Diving for a rat it spies.
Down it falls, and grabs the rat,
Kills and eats it, quick as that.

In the morning, you could see,
Several pellets by the tree.
Pellets with some parrot feet,
Beaks and claws of parakeet.

Great horned owls eat smaller things,
Some with fur and some with wings.
It is clear that these would eat,
Now and then a parakeet.

Do you think that we should judge?
Say "that's wrong," and hold a grudge?
After all, let's not be hasty.
Most of us think chicken's tasty.

Then one day the owls made peace.
No more parrots did they eat.
No one knows what made them change-
It was really very strange.

Owls can't build a nest, I've heard.
They steal from another bird.
Possibly they took a nest,
Ate the owners - left the rest.

19

Most of March, the neighbors see,
One owl sitting patiently,
Right in sight, for all to see
On a nest, high in the tree.

"Would you look!" the neighbors gasp.
"What will it be next, I ask?
Owls in Bridgeport! Did you ever."
Say the neighbors. "Well. I never!"

Late one night there was a cry,
Sort of mournful, sort of high.
Neighbors rolled their windows down,
Shutting out the dreadful sound.

"What on earth was that strange yowl?
Was it beast or was it fowl?"
Neighbors asked, that Tuesday morning,
Drinking coffee, blinking, yawning.

"Look up there," a young boy said.
"What's that fluffy little head?
Could that be a baby owl?
Could that be what made that howl?"

21

$\mathcal{H}$e picked up a stone and threw,
Just to see what it would do.
"Don't," the neighbors cried. "Don't try it.
Those owls need their peace and quiet."

Parrots soon began their din.
Everybody went back in.
Ruffle flew, and Coo just fluttered,
And inside, the neighbors muttered.

"Baby great horned owls. My word.
Here in Bridgeport. It's absurd.
Owls and parrots. Side by side.
What a **tree**," they smile, with pride.

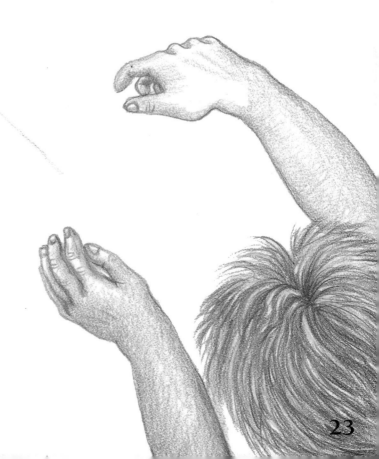

23

Meanwhile, spring brings buds and flowers.
Neighbors watch the tree for hours.
Coo is busy bringing food
For a growing parrot brood.

Ruffle stays and Ruffle sits.
On three eggs, she barely fits.
Thirty days she waits with Coo
Then the chicks come pecking through.

Parrot chicks, to you or me,
Might be quite a sight to see.
Naked, helpless, blind and small,
These newborns aren't cute at all!

But to Coo, and also Ruff,
These new chicks are cute enough.
Coo brings buds and sapling bark,
Coo brings food from dawn to dark.

25

*H*igher up, the owlet grows.
Frequently, he's mobbed by crows.
Crows, who hate all owls with passion,
Fly at him, dive-bomber fashion.

Baby owl grows rapidly.
So do Coo and Ruffle's three.
Mother owl brings squirrel or rat.
Little owl grows very fat.

Sometimes mother leaves him, crying.
"Hoooo," he howls, as if he's dying.
"Hoooo-doo - that's my name," he sings,
Struts about and flaps his wings.

Baby owl has golden eyes,
Rings of gold that mesmerize.
He's been practicing to fly.
Any day now, he will try.

First he takes some little hops,
At a lower branch he stops,
Climbs back up the tree, and then,
Hoo Doo hops and climbs again.

Then one evening, Hoo Doo flies
Out into the star-filled skies.
Every evening after that
He goes hunting mouse or rat.

"Where's that baby?" "Where's that mother?"
Asks one neighbor of another.
"They've gone hunting," he replied.
"Better lock the cat inside."

"What a tree," another howls.
"We've got parrots, crows and owls.
Here in Bridgeport! Did you ever."
Say the neighbors. "Well. I never!"

29

Why with many trees so near,
Did these parrots all come here?
What brought great horned owls here too?
Can it be they liked the view?

Can it be that graceful tree
Wanted friends for company?
How can owls and parrots be
Side by side, in harmony?

These are questions we may pose,
But the answers, no one knows.
Life is full of mystery,
Like the owl and parrot tree.

Glossary

jealous	suspicious, watchful, wanting something all to oneself
preen	a bird cleans its feathers with its beak
display	birds show off their feathers
jaguar	a big, spotted jungle cat, very rare and endangered
courting	to try to get another's affection
jungle	a thick, deep forest
frantic	wild, desperate
lush	rich, covered with growth
burly	big and heavy
flock	a group of birds
grimy, gritty	dirty
bellow	yell loudly
drenching	heavy downpour
din	loud noise
sapling	young trees or bushes
mesmerize	to put under a spell, hypnotize

Illustrations left to right:

Page 4: • "Cotton-top" Marmosets
  • Jaguar
  • Butterflies:
    Mesene Margaretta (orange)
    Lymnas Pixe (black)

Page 5: • Ring-tailed Lemur
  • Coral Snake

The real Owl and Parrot Tree

The Humane Society of the U.S., a nonprofit organization founded in 1954, and with a constituency of over a million and a half persons, is dedicated to speaking for animals, who cannot speak for themselves. The HSUS is devoted to making the world safe for animals through legal, educational, legislative and investigative means. The HSUS believes that humans have a moral obligation to protect other species with which we share the Earth. For information on The HSUS, call: 202 452-1100.

Text and Illustrations Copyright © 1993 by Randy Houk

Printed by Horowitz Rae
Designed by Anita Soos Design, Inc.

Published by The Benefactory, Inc.
One Post Road, Fairfield, CT 06430
The Benefactory produces books, tapes, and toys that foster animal protection and environmental preservation. Call: 203-255-7744

Printed on recycled paper
10 9 8 7 6 5 4 3 2

ISBN 1-882728-02-5
Printed in the U.S.A.

32